Hana & The Hairy Bod Rapper

by Dr Leema Jabbar

illustrated by Pearly L.

This book is dedicated to my favourite SWVs-
Sisters With Voices & *Sass*-
Neema and Shaheen
&
to my PC World- Pete,
You are my *ROCK*!

Hana was a bright and brilliant girl.

She loved to dance tango, tumble and twirl!

She glanced at her arm
and put it straight down.
'It really is hairy'
she thought with a frown!

From that moment on,
her mind was a blur.
All she could see was fleece,
fluff and fur!

She pulled down her sleeves
and kept her arms crossed,
Stopped dancing
and skipping,
totally lost.

When she got home,
she ran straight to her room,
Her spirit and spark replaced
with her gloom.

She cried,
"Mirror, mirror on the wall,
Who's the hairiest of them all?
I know it's me, how I hate my hair,
I wish it were gone,
It's just not fair!"

All of a sudden, the lighting went weird,
An explosion of glitter, then something appeared!
Hana was stunned, began rubbing her eyes,
The fairy before her was such a surprise!

"Who are you?" she asked, her voice a bit hoarse.
"Why, I'm your Hairy Bod Rapper - of course!
Flew here to help cos I heard you wishin',
To rap you this tune, my number one mission!"

"Your hair is a blessing and I'll tell you why,
You're lucky to have it so please do not cry.
I'll tell you a secret that you'll want to hear,
Your mind will be blown but you gotta come near!"

"We've all got a rhythm that beats within,
To groove you along and make ya head spin.
Each one of your hairs has a big part to play,
Makes you skip diddy skip and swivel or sway.
But how does that music come so alive?
I'll tell you how and expect a high five!"

"You rock a hair band all over you see,
And that's no mean feat, you gotta agree?"

"Your tempo is set
by banging base drums,
You feel it inside you
when the time comes."

"Strings vibrate from the electric guitar,
Pulsing right through you, you'll feel like a star!"

"Trumpets and trombones are all on the list.
There's so much more, but you get the gist!"

"So now you see
why you're so good at dance,
It's thanks to your hair band,
so give it a chance!"

"And if you look closely, in others you'll see,
Alternate hair shades on that knobby knee.
Their Hair band's sound will be different to yours,
It's beautiful music, just with their own scores."

"The rhythm's divine by their own design,
So, no matter the vibe, they'll surely shine.
Football or fencing, whatever you choose,
Own it and rock it and you'll never lose!"

"Now if you still want me to grant you your wish,
I'll magic your hairs gone with one simple swish."
"No way!" Hana said, "I'm one of a kind,
The truth of my hair band has blown my mind!
I totally love it and feel really proud,
I'm not ashamed, I'll shout it out loud!"

Hearing those words,
the Hairy Bod Rapper flew,
As Hana was happy
and no longer blue.

Next day at school she had got back her swagger,
So much to tell but she wasn't a bragger.

She surveyed the scene, a smile on her face,
So many jazzing in such a small space.

Susie the swimmer
was strumming away,

Reggie the runner
was tapping all day,

Ari the artist was humming a tune,

Dillis the dinner lady drumming her spoon!

So keen to learn and now she knew why!
When the teacher next asked,
she rocked her hand high!

And this time when Dee
was about to point out,

Hana whooped...

"MY HAIR BAND IS WHAT IT IS ALL ABOUT !!!'

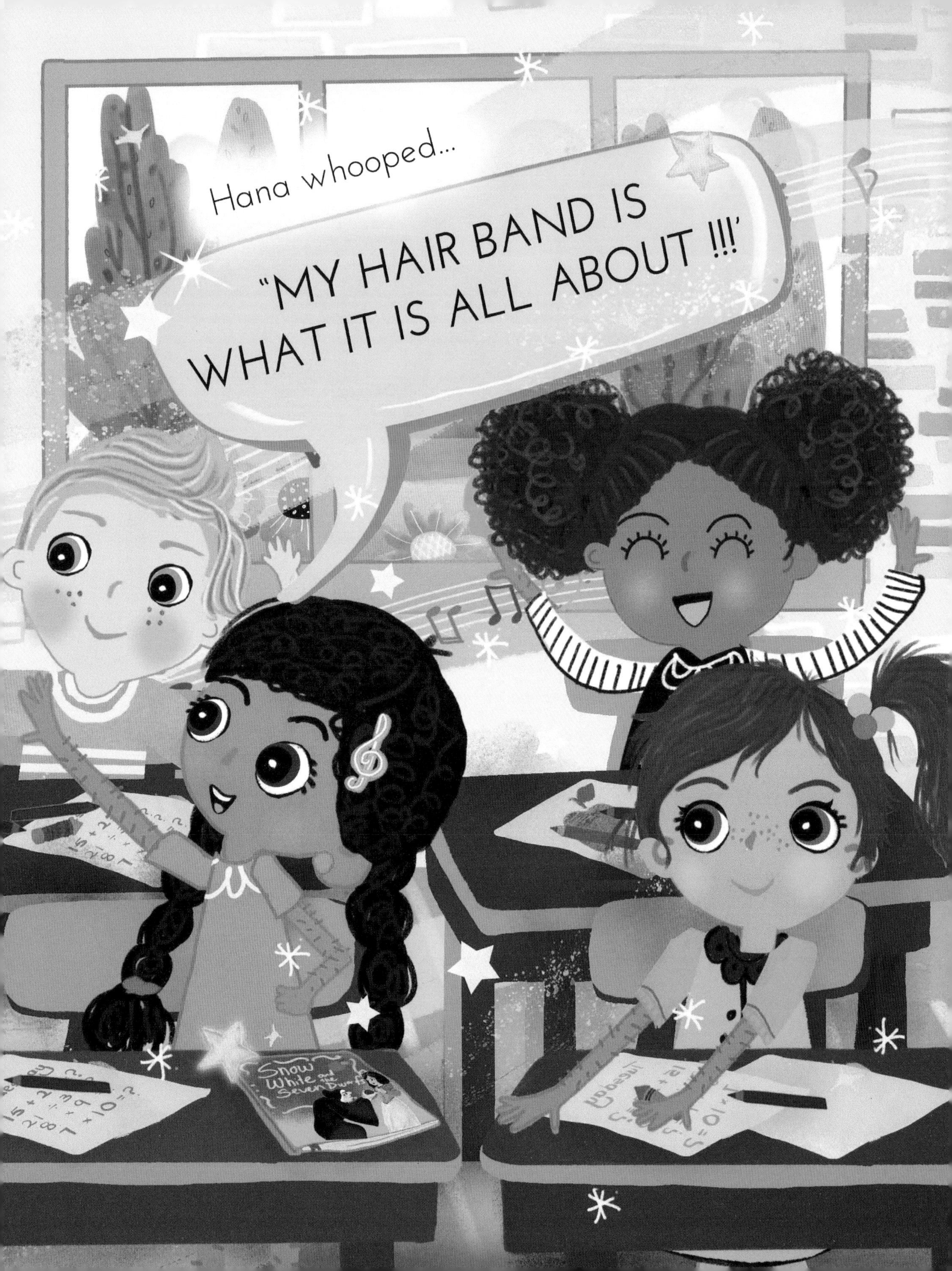

"Throw your arms up in the air,
Wave 'em like you just don't care
Don't just stand there, bust a move
Hairy limbs are in the groove!"

Printed in Great Britain
by Amazon